LEVI

ALL THE SINGLE DADS BOOK THREE

SADIE KING

These single dad hotties are fiercely protective and will do anything for the ones they love.

The series features grumpy single dads, secret billionaires, shy neighbors, and men turned obsessive by the curvy heroines who capture their hearts.

Each book in the series is a standalone but best enjoyed together. And look out for your favorite characters from Maple Springs popping in for cameo appearances.

All the Single Dads

Jaxon – Kali & Jaxon

Jake – Fiona & Jake

Levi – Aria & Levi

Brock – Olive & Brock

Anton – Eden & Anton

Xavier – Angela & Xavier

LEVI

ALL THE SINGLE DADS BOOK THREE

Aria

I need routine in my life. Not the wild and unpredictable neighbor who can't even keep his lawn trimmed.

We shared a kiss one wild night, and then he left.

Now he's back, and my body is going crazy. He makes my skin heat and my pulse flutter. I'm in danger of losing control and that scares me.

I need control in my life; I need order. And that means banishing my wild neighbor for good.

Levi

My uptight neighbor with the pouty lips and curvy hips… She's nervous as hell and sexy as sin.

The night I finally kissed her was the same night I got the call that changed my life forever.

I had to leave in a hurry.

But now I'm back and I want my neighbor for my wife. No matter how skittish she is, she will be mine.

ARIA

There are six roses, three red and three white. They're leftovers from work that are starting to brown at the edges. I can't sell them like this, but if I pull off the outer petals, they'll look fresh for another day or two.

I choose a vase with a slim neck, so they'll keep bunched together, and slide the stems in one by one, carefully inspecting each one for irregularities and snipping off untidy leaves.

I'm inspecting the last stem when I hear it.

The distinctive hum of a Harley Davidson.

The rose slips through my fingers and falls to the kitchen counter, a thorn slicing through my flesh.

Blood drips onto the counter but I barely notice. I'm too fixated on the motorcycle that's weaving slowly up the street.

My heartbeat grows loud in my ears as I watch the bike slow down at my driveway.

He's back

The bike cuts across my lawn, churning mud into my freshly-planted grass seed before it veers into the neighbor's driveway.

He's back and he's already destroying my carefully cultivated lawn.

Indignation rises in my chest. I pull up the corner of the net curtain to get a better look, and that's when I notice I'm bleeding.

"Shoot!"

Deep red droplets splash onto the kitchen counter. I pop my finger in my mouth and suck the wound. The metallic taste makes me dizzy and brings back a memory.

It's a muggy summer evening and I'm standing under the magnolia tree. He pushes himself against me, his leather pants causing a delicious friction against my cotton skirt.

His lips crash into mine. So urgent, so demanding, that his teeth cut my lip. The taste of blood mixes with too much sweet wine and the smell of leather.

Oh god, that kiss. We'd bickered since he'd moved in and, in a moment of insanity, I kissed him.

The memory makes me dizzy, and I feel a sensation in my core - a quiver that runs between my legs and gives me the urge to pee.

My breathing goes erratic, and I know I need to pull myself out of this before I have a panic attack.

But I can't take my eyes off the figure on the bike. Levi, my neighbor, who disrupted my equilibrium and then disappeared. He pulls his helmet off and shaggy dark hair cascades around his face. His beard has gotten longer, more wild, more unruly.

He turns in his seat and that's when I notice there's someone on the back of the bike.

I gasp as I reach for my phone, speed dialing Jenny, my best friend. She's always the person I call when I need to be talked down from the edge.

She answers on the first ring, and I don't bother with hellos.

"He's back."

There's silence on the other end.

I carry on, frustrated. "My neighbor."

"The motorbike dude?"

"Yes, and he just ran over my new grass seed on that oversized heap of junk."

"The guy you kissed last summer?"

"That was a mistake."

She snorts. "When is kissing a hot single guy ever a mistake?"

I roll my eyes even though she can't see me.

"You know why. He's loud and noisy and, and…" I search for the words, trying to recall what about him I hated so much. Then I remember – coming and going when he pleased on his motorbike with no routine, letting the lawn get high when it shouldn't, playing his guitar on the porch. "…unpredictable," I finish. "He's unpredictable."

Jenny goes silent. She knows how much I need order in my life. She's known me since we were kids.

Some people think I'm uptight and regimented. Jenny knows it's that I need things to be ordered. It's the only way I can make sense of life.

"And he's got a kid."

"What?"

"On the back of the bike. There's a kid."

I'm not sure why the kid has me feeling so indignant. I always knew my neighbor would be back one day, but I never expected him to bring a kid with him on the back of his bike. It's not what I've been expecting, and I don't know how to handle it.

"Whose kid is it?"

"I don't know. He left exactly 23 weeks ago, and he never mentioned a kid. Now he's got a kid on the back of the bike."

"Maybe he's giving him a lift."

I peer out the window at them, smiling as they get off the Harley.

"I don't think so, the kid is wearing bike gear."

"Maybe he abducted him."

I hear the teasing in her voice.

"Don't joke with me, Jenny. I'm hyperventilating here."

Her voice goes serious. "Okay, Aria. Take some deep breaths."

I do as she says, taking a moment to breathe in and out.

As the breath flows out of me, my anxiety starts to ease.

After a moment, Jenny speaks again.

"So, have you talked to him?"

"No, he's only just pulled up. He made me cut my finger."

She snorts. "Aria, if a man has that much effect on you, it usually means you like him and you should give him a chance.

"No way. I told you, I'm going to be single for life. I'm happy as I am. I don't want anyone, and I don't need anyone."

I can tell she's smiling through the phone.

"Okay, hon, if that's what you want. I just think maybe you should keep an open mind."

I pull the curtain back and watch him. He puts an arm around the boy's shoulders as he leads him up the steps toward the house.

He unlocks the door, and the boy goes inside first. Levi is about to follow when he stops. He turns around and his gaze sweeps my property, landing on the kitchen window.

I drop the curtain and take a step back.

"Shoot."

"What is it?"

"He just caught me looking at him."

I watch in horror as he strides across his overgrown lawn and onto my pristine one.

"He's coming this way. He just walked all over my grass seed."

Jenny doesn't bother to hide her laughter.

"What should I do?"

"Get the hell off the phone and go talk to him!"

2

LEVI

Six months I've been gone. Six long months away from Aria, my uptight neighbor who managed to wind her way into my heart despite having a go at me for every neighborhood folly I committed or thought of committing.

I started letting my lawns grow just so I could hear her tell me off. Her hands on her hips, lip quivering with indignation. My gentle teasing only infuriated her more and I loved it.

At the neighborhood street party last summer, I cornered her and kissed her like she needed to be kissed. She fought me for a moment before giving in, her body pressed against mine, hips grinding against me. She pulled away almost as quickly, but not before I saw the need in her eyes.

I let her go that night, thinking there would be plenty of time for her to come round to the idea that we were meant to be together. But later that night I got the call. And my life hasn't been the same since.

I stride up to her steps and ring the doorbell. I know she saw me return and I don't want to waste any time saying hello and explaining why I left right after that kiss.

She opens the door tentatively, like she doesn't know it's me on the other side. She is the picture of innocence in a flowing skirt and jumper, her breasts pushing against the fabric in a way I can't help but notice. Her blonde hair is pulled back in a neat ponytail showing off her round face and pale blue eyes. Her cheeks are flushed, and she looks indignant.

"You ran over my grass seed."

I grin because it's good to hear her chide me, good to know she hasn't changed.

"It'll help push them into the soil, I reckon."

Her hands go to her hips. "Your lawn hasn't been mowed in 23 weeks."

Now I really do smile as I lean against the door frame. "You were counting how long I was gone?"

The color rises on her cheeks.

"Don't be ridiculous. You know I count everything."

Which is true, I do know that. What I know about my strange, beautiful neighbor is she's not just uptight, she's downright crazy. But I've seen a lot of crazy and at least I can understand this. She obviously needs order to put right whatever trauma she's had in her life.

So instead of an uptight neighbor, I see a vulnerable woman who needs healing and a man to love her. I just need to convince her I'm that man. Especially since my life got a whole lot more complicated these past few months.

"I'm sorry I left like I did, straight after what happened."

Her eyes flicker before her expression goes hard.

"It doesn't matter. I don't really remember what happened."

She's still angry with me, and I don't blame her. You don't kiss a woman like that and then leave.

"Something came up and I had to leave quickly, but I'm back now. For good."

My eyes hold hers and I try to convey all my feelings into my expression. How I've thought about her every day when I was away, and how every night... that kiss kept me going through a lot of lonely nights. But now she's here in front of me, her mouth in a thin line and her eyes cold, and that kiss seems a long way away.

"I shouldn't have left straight after I kissed you."

"I don't really recall it. I'd had a lot of wine." She turns away, unable to hold my gaze, and sweeps a nonexistent tendril of hair from her cheek. That's when I see the blood.

I catch her hand in mine.

"You're bleeding."

She tries to pull her hand back, but I hold it. Her slender fingers are soft in my rough, mechanic hands. I lift the finger to my lips and slide it into my mouth, tasting her blood, and sucking at it gently.

She gasps, her mouth falling open in a surprised 'oh', that makes my dick ache.

My mouth moves down her hand kissing her fingers, her palm.

"Aria…" I murmur into her flesh. "I've thought of nothing but you."

Her gaze is on mine, and I see desire fighting with something else. The something else wins. She snatches her hand away, and I feel the loss of her like a coldness in my heart.

"I haven't thought of you at all. It was a mistake what happened last summer, and it won't be repeated."

I reach for her, and she flinches. Her breathing is growing heavy, and I can see I'm causing her stress. I back away with my hands up.

"Okay, okay. I'll go if that will make you happy."

She calms down slightly, my nervous filly. I'll back away today, but I know she will eventually be mine.

"Um, dad?" The voice comes from across the lawn.

Aria's eyes go wide as she takes in Josh. He looks bewildered and unsure, a twelve-year-old who's been transplanted to a new home.

"I didn't know you had a son." She's curious, which I take to be a good sign, a sign she cares.

"Neither did I."

Aria looks confused and I don't blame her. It confused the hell out of me, too.

"I'll tell you all about it over dinner tonight."

Her expression hardens. "It makes no difference to me if you have a hundred children. I'm not interested, Levi. I wasn't interested six months ago, and I'm not interested now."

It's harsh, and I try not to flinch.

"I'm not interested in any man. I just want a quiet life with a respectful neighbor. If you really want to make me happy, you can start by mowing your lawn."

With that set down, she goes inside and shuts the door.

I cross the lawn and take the steps to my door

two at a time. Josh raises his eyebrows at me with a look well beyond his years.

"Who was that?"

"That, son, is my future wife."

3

ARIA

I'm in such a rush to get to work the next morning that I don't notice the sound of the lawn mower until I step outside.

I freeze on the top step.

Levi is mowing the lawn with his shirt off, his muscles glistening in the morning sun. There's a ripple up his arm as he pushes the mower forward.

It's the first time I've seen his bare body, and I'm mesmerized. It's all hard muscle and ink. The designs of his tattoo dance as he moves.

My body flushes hot. It's suddenly difficult to breathe.

He pivots at the end of the line and turns back in my direction. His hand raises in a cheery salute the minute his eyes land on me, that stupid lazy grin on his face giving the impression he knows what I'm thinking.

I drag my eyes away from him and will my feet to move down the steps to the car. My body is having a mini rebellion and I can't bear to look at him again or I'll have a panic attack. The man is all man and muscle and danger.

Keeping my eyes averted, I get into the car and start the engine.

He's moved down to the strip between our houses and as I reverse, I get a glimpse of his toned body in the rear view.

I almost hit the letterbox I'm so distracted.

He gives me another wave and I purposefully ignore him.

Of all the times to mow the lawn, he chose to do it when I'm going to work. He couldn't have waited to do it when I was out? And he couldn't have kept his shirt on? It's as if he's purposefully trying to disrupt my world.

I'm still fuming when I push open the door to the florist shop I co-own with Jenny. She takes one look at me and frowns.

"Uh oh, what's up?"

"He was mowing the lawn this morning."

Her expression changes.

"That's good though, right? That's what you

wanted."

It's true. She's listened to me complain about his wild lawn for the past six months – but that's not the point.

"With his shirt off."

Her eyes dance with mirth. "Oh man, so he's showing you the goods, huh?"

I put my bag in its cubbyhole and neaten up the piles of colored paper under the countertop.

"I don't want him to 'show me the goods'. I want him to be a good neighbor and leave me alone."

I can feel the heat rising in my cheeks.

"Are you sure about that?"

I turn to Jenny and fix her with a stare. She knows what I went through; she knows why I've never let any man come close, why I've never had a serious boyfriend.

"Yes, I'm sure about that, and you know why."

Her expression softens and she puts a hand on my arm. "I know, hon. I know your reasons. But maybe it's time to heal those wounds, and this guy might be the place to start."

I know she means well, but I don't want to heal my wounds. This is who I am, and I've accepted that.

"I'll always be single and that's fine with me."

She gives me a comforting smile. At least I know

whatever happens, I'll always have Jenny to understand.

The bell above the door jangles, signaling our first customer. I put the events of the morning behind me and put on my best smile.

It's a few days later and I'm driving home from a busy day at the shop. I've managed to avoid Levi by only leaving the house for work and going in and out as quickly as I can.

He hasn't tried to speak to me again, but I've noticed he's taking care of the jobs around his yard that had been neglected. The lawn is short and neat, the fence has been repaired, and he's weeded around most of the flower beds.

In the evenings, I've seen him on the porch with his kid, strumming guitar and singing.

I'm curious about the boy. He never mentioned a son, but I guess I never gave him much of a chance to tell me anything at all about himself.

I'm almost home when my nostrils flare at a strange smell. It's like burning and grease.

The car splutters just as I notice the engine light flash red.

"Shoot."

I pull over to the side of the road just as the car shivers to a halt; smoke coming out of the hood.

I get out and open the hood. Steam bursts out of the radiator and I jump back just in time. I don't know much about cars, but I know this isn't good.

I'm leaning over the engine, wondering what the hell to do when I hear the distinctive hum of a Harley.

I don't need to look up to know it's Levi. He slows down and pulls up in front of my sad-looking car.

"Need a hand?"

I give a feeble protest, Levi's the last person I want help from, but he's already off his bike and looking under the hood. A waft of leather and grease and fresh grass comes from his body.

My head spins and I take a quick step back, needing to put some space between us. To get away from him, away from the pull he has on me.

"Looks like the engine. I've got a mate who can tow it to his garage to take a look."

He's already got his phone out, making the call. I try to protest but he silences me with a finger in the air as he talks to his mate.

"They'll come get it this evening," he finally says as he pulls the phone from his ear.

My head is spinning. I need my car to get home

and I need to get home because it's Wednesday and Wednesday is the day I vacuum the house before making chicken casserole for dinner.

"But how will I get home?"

He gives me one of his lazy smiles and gestures towards his bike.

"I'll give you a lift."

He can't possibly mean on his bike – that noisy thing with no doors and no seatbelt. I shake my head and back away.

"No thanks. I'll walk."

He takes my elbow and I'm so surprised by the heat from his touch that before I realize what's happening, I've let him guide me over to the bike.

"Jump on."

I can't possibly get on the back of that dangerous thing, but his hand runs to the small of my back and I'm propelled forward by his touch.

"Come on, climb on."

For a moment, I wonder what it must be like not to be so anxious all the time. What it must be like to be one of those girls who would climb on the back of a man's motorbike and let her hair catch in the wind as she speeds through town.

But I'm not that girl and I'm not getting on that bike.

"There's no helmet."

He shrugs. "It's only a few blocks. I'll go slow."

My mind spins. I can smell his scent and he's so close to me that my heart's racing. My breathing grows shallow and he must sense it because he puts an arm around me, gentler than I'd expect from a man his size.

"You're okay, Aria," he whispers. "Just breathe."

I close my eyes and lean into his chest. With his strong arm around me, I immediately feel calmer.

I stay there for a moment and when I open my eyes, he's looking at me with a softness I've not seen before.

"Now can you get on the damn bike and let me take you home?"

4

LEVI

She's holding my waist with a vise-like grip and her head is pressed against my back. No doubt her eyes are closed tight even though I'm doing less than twenty miles per hour.

I can't believe I finally got her onto the back of my bike. And now that I have her, I intend to make the most of it.

We're approaching the intersection but instead of turning down our street, I keep going straight.

I feel her head snap up off my back. She's saying something I can't make out, but I guess is along the lines of, "Where the fuck are you taking me?"

There's no point trying to talk to her while we're moving, my baby purrs far too loud. So, I just drive on, out of town and along a winding path that leads up the hill to the maple forest the town was named after.

Her grip never relaxes but after a few minutes her head rests again on my back. I feel the heat of her behind me. Even through my biking leathers, her warm body heats me right to the core.

It's another five minutes before we turn off onto the dirt track that's too small for cars. I take it slow as we weave along the track dodging low tree branches and potholes. Eventually, we come to a clearing that overlooks the farmland on the east side of town.

I used to come up here with my buddy David whose family owns one of the farms below. But that's not what I want Aria to see.

I kill the engine and the only sounds are the birds and the wind rustling the trees. I already know she's going to be angry with me, so I take my time getting off the bike.

When I finally risk a glance at her face, sure enough, she's looking at me like I stole her first born.

"You were supposed to be take me home."

Her irate look, pouty lips, and flashing eyes makes the blood rush to my dick. She has no idea what effect she has on me, and that's what makes it all the sweeter.

"I want to show you something."

I hold out a hand to help her off the bike, but she stays put.

"I want you to take me home."

She folds her arms and her lips quiver. I can see there's something bigger going on here.

"Baby girl, what is it?" I'm all concern, and she must pick up on that because she looks up at me then, her eyes wide and vulnerable.

"I don't like surprises, Levi. I like routine, and this is breaking my routine."

She's playing with the rings on her fingers, and I can tell she's anxious. I've been a dumbass and upset her.

My arms go around her and she slumps against me.

"I'm sorry, baby girl. I didn't think." Her hair smells like fruity shampoo, and I run my lips over the top of her head.

"Take some deep breaths. You're safe with me."

I give her all the time she needs until I feel her breathing relax and her body stops shaking.

I crouch down so I'm eye level with her. "There's something I really want to show you, then I'll take you straight home, I promise."

She looks at me for a long moment like she's weighing the decision. Finally, she nods, and I let out a breath I didn't know I was holding.

I help her off the bike, keeping my hand in hers as I lead her down a narrow path to a rock face. We shuffle round the side of the rock and below us is a sea of purple.

She gasps when she sees it. Her hands go to her face in delight and I know I've done the right thing.

"The lavender fields."

"Yup"

There's a large lavender farm on the edge of town and when they're in bloom it's like a purple ocean.

There's a large flat boulder nearby and we shimmy up, keeping the lavender below us.

Her breathing is back to normal, her eyes are shiny, and she's smiling – which is a relief to see. I want to ask her about her anxiety, but I guess she'll tell me when she's ready. Right now, it's time I gave her some explanations.

"I didn't know I had a son until I got a phone call six months ago."

She keeps looking out at the fields, and I take it as a sign to go on.

"It was the same night we kissed, after I took you home."

Her face remains passive, but a telltale blush creeps up her neck.

"I was with Josh's mother, Carol, for a time. It

was years ago, and we parted on friendly terms. We didn't stay in touch, and she never told me she was pregnant."

I check Aria's expression but she's not giving anything away.

"It wasn't until I got that call that I even knew Josh existed. Carol was sick and she wanted Josh to meet his father. I was skeptical, but a test proved he's mine.

"Carol had an aggressive cancer and I stayed near them until she passed. It gave Josh time to get to know me, and allowed me to be there for him. Because I knew as soon as I met him that I wanted him in my life."

"That must have been hard for him."

Her concern is genuine, and it goes straight to my heart.

"He's been through a lot. His mom was into some bad things, she ran with a bad crowd, but she was still his mom. He's with me now, though, and I'll do everything I can to do right by him."

She turns to me, and her expression is soft, as tender as I've ever seen her.

"That's noble."

"Hell, it's not noble, I missed twelve years of his life. I want to make up for that. That kid's been through enough, I want to give him a home."

"Why did you break up with his mother?"

The question takes me by surprise. Was that jealousy I detected in her tone? I scan her face, but all I see is curiosity.

"It was never serious. Carol was too wild, too unstable. I was with her for only a few months and she told me she was on the pill. I knew we weren't right together, and I wanted to leave that life behind. I prefer my women more… predictable."

I give her a pointed look and her eyes meet mine. Her lips part and I know in that instant I'm going to kiss her.

5

ARIA

I don't know if it's the lavender blowing gently in the wind below us, the sound of the rustling leaves, or the scent of worn leather and grease that's oh-so-slowly becoming familiar to me, but I feel a calmness wash over me. It's like I'm safe here and nothing can hurt me. My heartbeat slows. I close my eyes and lean closer toward Levi, giving in to the pull of him.

His lips press to mine and it's as gentle as the breeze on the lavender fields below. I sigh, a sound like the wind, and let myself relax, let myself be taken along by the slow sweet kiss. His lips mold to mine, his tongue gentle and tentative.

His hands cup my cheeks and I feel myself giving in to this man my body craves although I don't understand why.

For one long, lovely moment, my body and mind relax.

Then his hand moves down my neck, and my pulse quickens. There's a pull in my core and a rush of heat between my legs. My body is doing things I can't control.

I feel dizzy as the memory overtakes me.

Hiding in the closet as the sounds of their arguing erupt down the hall. The sound of a fist connecting with flesh and the muffled cry of shock from my mother. Then the steady whack, whack, whack of fists as my mother took a silent beating. Holding in her pain so I wouldn't hear. But I did hear. I heard it all.

They pretended the next morning that mom had had another fall, or she'd been in an accident, or she'd slipped on the steps. And I pretended to believe.

The way she darted around him tentatively for a few weeks, jumpy and nervous. Then the bruises would fade, the cuts would heal. She'd smile again, give him her love and he'd put his arm around her and call her his little dove.

I'd hear them singing together, laughing, loving, as if the beatings had never happened. And then they would happen again. Sure as the sun comes up in the morning, he'd beat her again.

It's a part of love that I'm not willing to accept.

The image of my mom's bruised face comes into my head, and I pull away with a gasp. My eyes are wide, shocked at how I almost let myself get pulled into him, this man with strong arms who could crush me if he wanted to.

He sees my alarmed look and his face is a picture of concern.

"Aria, it's okay to want to kiss me, you know."

I shake my head. He'll never understand. It's *not* okay. I can't deny I have feelings for him and that's what's so dangerous. I don't want love. Love leads to bruises and trips to the hospital and lying to your kids through broken teeth.

"Take me home, please."

I slide off the rock and start walking down the path.

I hear him behind me and his arm reaches out to spin me around.

"Whatever has happened to you, whatever you're scared of, I'm not going to hurt you."

I shake him off and keep walking because he'll never understand.

I get on the back of the bike and wait for him to catch up.

"I'll take you home," he says. "But whenever you're ready, I'm here for you."

I want to believe him as we ride through the streets back to town. I want to believe he's not like my stepdad. But I can't be sure. It's safer to stick to what I know.

It's safer to stick to my routines and my single, safe life. It's lonely, but at least I'm safe.

6

LEVI

I slam my fist into the punching bag and Josh jumps out the way as it swings toward him.

"Whoa, Dad, you're gonna hit me."

"Sorry, buddy."

We're doing a few rounds with the punching bag in the basement, but I've got so much pent-up anger at whoever made my girl so nervous that I'm taking it out on the bag. I stop and wipe the sweat from my face.

"You have a go and I'll spot you," I say, as Josh raises his gloved hands. "Remember to keep your hands up and your chin down."

I thought it would be hard suddenly having a kid in my life, but the truth is, I love having Josh around. He's a good sparring buddy, not bad on the guitar, and has a healthy interest in bikes. At least his good-for-nothing mother did something right.

"Is it girl trouble?"

The question takes me by surprise, and I let the bag go just has he swings. I dodge out of the way before it hits me.

"What do you know about girl trouble?" I ask with a smile.

"I know you're moping around like a puppy who's had its nuts chopped off."

I give a surprised laugh. I don't know where he gets these expressions, but he does make me chuckle. "What do you know about it?"

"Is it that neighbor?"

I nod. "Yeah."

"Playing hard to get?"

I frown. "I don't think she's playing, buddy. She's a complex woman and I seem to make her nervous. Sometimes you've got to go easy, take things slow in new relationships."

Josh shrugs. "Or you got to go in there and take what you want."

Oh boy, he's got a lot to learn. "No son, you *never* take what you want from a woman."

He rolls his eyes. "Yeah, I know, I know, you need consent before you do it."

My eyebrows shoot into my forehead. "What do you know about doing it?"

"Dad, I'm twelve."

My head is spinning. What does a twelve-year-old know about sex? I've never even talked to him about sex or condoms or how to treat a woman right. I'm suddenly overwhelmed by the responsibilities of raising a son into a man.

He puts a hand on my shoulder. "Don't worry, Dad. I haven't done it yet."

Relief floods me. "Good, cause there's some things we need to talk about."

He rolls his eyes at me again.

"Later. Right now we need to talk about you." He pokes a gloved fist at my chest.

Since our kiss at the lookout, I've pulled back with Aria, given her space. "I'm giving her time to cool off before my next move," I admit. "But to be honest, I don't know what that next move should be."

"You need to go over there and tell her how you feel. Tell her you're her man now."

Great, I'm taking relationship advice from a twelve-year-old.

"Thanks kid, but I think I got it."

He pulls his gloves off in frustration. "You're not taking me seriously."

Right, because he's twelve. What could he possibly teach me?

"Some girls like to be chased and some girls like to be told. It seems you've tried chasing, so now you need to tell her how it's gonna be, that you're her man now, and she's gonna come live with us and have your babies."

I snort at the last remarks but he's deadly serious. Maybe this kid has more of a vested interest than just making his old man happy. Maybe he needs a new mom.

I lean forward and put a hand on Josh's shoulder.

"I do want Aria to come and live with us, but I won't ask her to until you're ready. You're my family now, and I want to do what's right by you."

"Then go get her, Dad. The sooner she gets here, the better. I mean, I like boxing and playing guitar and stuff, but…"

He looks down and swipes quickly at his eyes. I know what he's thinking. He misses his mom.

"You miss her, huh?"

He nods. "Yeah."

My heart goes out to the little guy. He's been through so much.

"Plus, you're kinda stinky. It'd be nice to have a woman in the house."

"You little…" I take a playful swipe at him, but he darts out of the way.

"Don't waste time with me, Dad. Go talk to her!"

7

ARIA

The doorbell makes me jump and I drop the plate I'm cleaning into the sink, splashing water over the counter.

"Shoot."

My hands tremble as I run the cloth over the counter, guiding the water back into the sink.

I've been a nervous wreck for the last three days. Ever since that kiss on the rock where I nearly let myself go, nearly let myself get swept away.

I know it's Levi at the door before I even see him. Surprisingly, the knowing makes me feel calm, stills my breathing. I pull the door open and he's leaning against the doorframe, just as I knew he would be, with a lazy smile and sparkling eyes.

He's holding a bunch of daisies, the large wild ones that grow at the borders of his garden.

"I picked these for you."

The stems are uneven with fronds of leaves trailing at every angle. They're wild, like him. Like the feelings I have for him.

"Thank you."

I take the daisies, keeping my eyes downcast. I can barely stand to look at him in case my feelings overwhelm me.

"Aria…"

His hands clasp mine around the flowers and I gasp at his touch. It's electric and powerful.

He moves forward, pushing me backwards into the kitchen. I should stop him, I should push back, but as his body crashes into mine, I don't want to.

He kicks the door shut with his foot and backs me up against the kitchen counter.

"We're meant to be together, you and I."

He grinds the words out against my neck, his husky voice causing shivers to run over my body. His breath on my skin makes the hairs on my arms stand on end and sends shockwaves to my aching nipples.

I whimper against him, and his hand runs up my body, over my breasts, and to my chin.

He gently tilts my face so I'm forced to look him in the eye.

What I see makes my body ache. There's lust, but also kindness, protectiveness.

"I love you, Aria. You'll always be safe with me."

And in this moment, I believe him. I want to believe him. My body is aching under his touch, wanting more of him, all of him.

His lips crash into mine and I kiss him tentatively, then with passion.

This time, when the feelings wash over me, I let myself get carried away. I let my heart beat wildly and my blood pulse in my ears. I let the heat between my legs build as his hands strokes my panties.

When he slides them off and lifts me onto the counter, I even let him sink his fingers into me. And when the climax builds, I let it carry me away with an abandonment I've never felt before.

My eyes flicker open and he's watching me carefully with that lazy grin.

"More," I croak.

Because now that he's unlocked me, I want all of him. I want him inside me so bad.

He groans as I reach for his belt buckle.

"Aria, I'll be gentle with you, if that's what you need."

I shake my head because now that I've had a taste, now that I've let my body go, released it to abandonment, I feel powerful. I'm more in control than I have been for years. I want him to fuck me hard and rough and dirty.

I slide off the bench and sink to my knees, pulling him to the floor.

"You don't need to be gentle."

I flip over to my knees and pull up my skirt so he gets a view of my bare ass. He groans as he takes my ass in his hands, pulling the flesh apart.

I look at him over my shoulder as he rubs his hard cock over my entrance.

"It's my first time."

He freezes and I whimper pushing my hips back to feel his cock against me again.

"Oh, baby girl. We should go to the bedroom then."

But I can't wait. I'm too scared if I stop this moment, I'll never feel this calm, this in control again.

"No, take me here."

He runs his hand up my thigh and leans forward to kiss my neck.

"If that's what you want."

He whispers it into my ear and the heat of his breath makes me shudder in anticipation.

His dick runs over my entrance and then he's pushing inside.

There's a brief pain and then I adjust to him, my

body making room for his girth. Then he's filling me up, claiming me as his and giving my body what it needs in return.

My hands glide down to my clit and as he thrusts, I stroke myself, my fingers curling around his balls as I rub my clit with my palm.

The feeling builds again, like I'm on a cliff edge. It's terrifying and wonderful all at once. And this time, I run toward the feeling, toward the cliff, and I jump off.

My body shakes as the orgasm wracks me, releasing tension that's built up for years.

Levi slams into me and then he's shaking, crying out my name. I feel his hot cum fill me up and spill over, trickling down my thighs.

I'm gliding through the air with him, peaceful and safe. And when I open my eyes, he's pulled me close to him, pulled me onto his lap in an embrace.

I feel calm, I feel safe, and I know I always will as long as I'm with him.

Five years later…

I hand the hotdog over to my wife and she immediately takes a large bite.

"Mmmm, thank you," she mumbles through the mouthful. A dribble of mustard runs down her chin and I wipe it with my thumb.

She always has a huge appetite when she's pregnant.

Luckily, we're at a dirt bike meet with a well-stocked hot dog stand. It's the second one she's had today.

I offer the other one to our daughter, but she wrinkles her nose.

"No thanks, Daddy. It's stinky."

"Suit yourself." I ruffle her hair and take a bite of

the spare hot dog.

Aria shoves the last of her hotdog in her mouth and wipes her lips with a napkin. I slide my arm around her waist, and she leans into me, her head resting on my shoulder.

She so different from the uptight neighbor I met nearly six years ago. Now she's relaxed and calm and confident. She just needed to be healed – and our love did that for her.

Sure, she has bad days sometimes, but I know just what she needs to calm her down.

My hand slides down her back and I cup her buttocks in my palm, not caring who might see.

I know when her anxiety surfaces, when she starts to worry and needs order in her life. That's when only the joining of our bodies will help. When we make love, it's like she releases the tension. It calms her and brings her back to me.

The noise of revving engines intensifies, and our daughter jumps up and down excitedly.

"They're about to start."

We all lean forward trying to see the start of the course. It's the state dirt bike championship and Josh is racing in the final.

Now almost a man, he's inherited my love of bikes and recklessness.

The starting gun signals the start of the race. We

hear them before we see them, racing around the sharp corners of the course.

We're positioned near the end of the lap and when the bikes come into view, he's in the lead.

"Come on!" screams Aria. She jumps up and down with excitement and so does our daughter.

I wrap an arm around the both of them, content and happy as I watch my first-born ride into the lead.

WHAT TO READ NEXT

PROTECTING HIS BRAT

This brat needs to be taught a lesson, and I'll be the one to discipline her…

Since retiring from the special forces, I've set up a team of elite personal security guards.

But I wasn't expecting the daughter of my first client to be such a brat.

Adrianna thinks she can play me, but she needs to be taught a lesson.

I'll be the one to take her over my knee.

She needs to learn that the only game I'm playing is for keeps.

Protecting His Brat is an OTT age-gap romance featuring an older military hero and a young curvy virgin.

Keep reading for an exclusive excerpt.

PROTECTING HIS BRAT

CHAPTER ONE

Bronn

It's an unusual house. Box-shaped rooms, jutting out at odd angles, looking like building blocks a child has stuck together.

The sun glints off the floor to ceiling windows, making me wince even behind my sunglasses.

It doesn't look homely, the hard lines making it look uncomfortable, unwelcoming, like a fortress. I should know. I've been staring at it all fucking day.

A black Mercedes waits on the driveway, the chauffeur as bored as I am.

But I'm good at waiting. I learned it in the Army, how to be still while remaining alert and how to spring into action when needed.

All good traits to be a security guard, which is

about the only work I could find when I retired from the special forces.

Still, clients pay top dollar for ex-military, especially when you've been in the Green Berets.

Finally, the front door opens, and my client, Phillip Brooks, steps out.

His dark tailored suit contrasts with the sun gleaming off the white walls of the house. His wife stands in the doorway, twisting her hands nervously, looking at him with doleful eyes.

He slides an arm around her waist, and I look away as he embraces her. I feel a pang of regret. The military life never allowed me to settle down with a woman. I wonder what it's like to have someone to say goodbye to, someone to miss you when you're away.

He steps away, and she tugs on his sleeve, not wanting him to leave. Gently, he pries her hand off his arm and hurries down the stairs.

He stops next to me, and I get a whiff of bourbon and expensive aftershave.

"Don't let her leave the property."

I nod, letting him know I've understood his instructions.

My client explained the threat to me, the death threats he's been getting, his concern for his wife.

If someone had threatened my woman, I wouldn't

be fucking off and leaving her alone. But it's not for me to judge. From what I understand, when you're in the oil business, like my client is, threats are a part of life.

The chauffeur holds the door open for my client, and he slides into the waiting car.

There's a wrought iron gate at the entrance to the property, and I scan the area around it, making sure there's nothing suspect before we open the gates.

As the car circles around the drive, I catch movement on the road.

My skin prickles, and I'm instantly on high alert. A black car is driving slowly down the road, too slow to be going straight past.

I jog in front of the Merc, holding my hand out to stop them. My client ducks down in the back seat, protecting himself from whatever threat this might be.

The black car comes to a stop outside the gate. It's got tinted windows, so I can't see who's inside.

Every fiber of my body is alert, my blood thumping, ready to meet the threat. I pull my piece and aim it at the car, keeping my hand steady.

The back door of the car opens, and I train my gun on whatever's going to come out of there. I won't be the first to fire, but if someone attacks, I won't hesitate to shoot.

There's the flutter of bright fabric, a flash of tanned leg, and a young woman slides out of the backseat. She's wearing a short, floaty dress that comes halfway up her thick thighs. It dips at the front, displaying a full cleavage of soft breast.

My mouth waters, and there's a twitch in my pants. If this is how my clients' enemies attack, then I'm screwed.

She can't be a day over twenty, but my dick doesn't seem to mind the age gap.

The woman shuts the door behind her and saunters over to the gate.

She slides her large designer glasses down her nose and peers at me over the rim, unimpressed by the gun I've got pointed at her.

"If this is the welcome I get, I would have stayed away." Her voice is as pouty as her look. Sassy and sharp.

I've been trained to encounter all kinds of enemies but not an entitled brat with a sticky pink pout and a mane of golden hair clasping an overnight bag to her plus-sized chest.

A car door slams behind me.

"Put the gun down, Bronn."

I slowly lower my piece, but I can't tear my eyes away from the woman. She wraps both hands around the iron bars and leans forward rattling the gate.

"Open the gate, Daddy."

Her voice is whiny and petulant, like an overgrown toddler. Like a spoiled brat who needs some discipline.

My client strides forward, irritation in his voice. "You're supposed to be at college."

The woman tears one hand off the gate and swipes at her golden hair. "It was boring."

"Did you get kicked out?" My client's voice is clipped, his anger not quite disguised.

The woman gives him a sweet smile.

"I wanted to be here with you instead."

My client harumphs and pushes the code for the gate. It swings open, and the woman sashays through.

"I've got a business trip. You can stay here with your mother."

"Oh, great," mutters the woman, and even though I can't see behind her glasses, I'm sure she's rolling her eyes. If any kid of mine spoke about my wife like that, I'd tan their hide. But her father doesn't react.

"Don't give your mother any trouble," he barks at her. "I'll be back in ten days. You stay inside these gates and I'll deal with you when I get back."

The daughter does a slow twirl as if checking out

her surroundings. Her eyes rest on me, and my body tenses as she looks me up and down.

"Who's the heavy?" she asks her father as if I'm not there.

"I'm Bronn."

Both the woman and her father look at me in surprise. To them, I'm the hired help, the silent security guard. But this brat needs to learn some respect. If her father isn't teaching her ,then I will.

She slides the sunglasses onto her head, showing off her large brown eyes. There's a mischievous look in them as she saunters toward me.

"Hello, Bronn."

My cock lengthens despite myself. I shift uncomfortably, clasping my hands in front of my body, hiding what's going on in my pants.

"I'm Adrianna."

From a distance, she was beautiful, but up close, she takes my breath away. I literally can't breathe as I stare at her, transfixed by her dark, playful eyes.

Heat sweeps over me, and I feel unbalanced. A surge of protectiveness rushes through me, and one thought bangs into my brain.

Mine.

"Bronn's here to protect you and your mother. Do exactly as he says and don't do anything stupid."

She's so close to me I can smell her cherry-flavored lip balm and expensive floral soap.

"Oh. I'll do exactly what you tell me to do," she murmurs so only I can hear.

My gaze flicks to her lips, so full, so pouty—just the right size for my cock.

Then she flicks her hair and flounces up the driveway.

I am so fucked.

To keep reading visit:
mybook.to/ProtectingHisBrat

ABOUT THE AUTHOR

Sadie King is a USA Today Best Selling Author of short instalove romance.

She lives in New Zealand with her ex-military husband and raucous young son.

When she's not writing she loves catching waves with her son, running along the beach, and good wine, preferably drunk with a book in hand.

Keep in touch when you sign up for her newsletter. You'll even snag yourself a free short romance!

www.authorsadieking.com/free